Keep Rollin'

J

A Day with Jay

by Jay Armstrong

Illustrated by Deborah C. Johnson

A Day with Jay

Copyright © 2010 Jay Armstrong

This is a work of fiction. Names, characters, places, and incidents either are the product of the author's imagination or are used fictitiously. Any resemblance to actual persons, living or dead, events, or locales is entirely coincidental.

Manufactured in the United States of America

For information, please contact:

The P3 Press
16200 North Dallas Parkway, Suite 170
Dallas, Texas 75248

www.thep3press.com
972-248-9500
A New Era in Publishing™

ISBN-13: 978-1-933651-60-6
ISBN-10: 1-933651-60-1
LCCN: 2009912515

Author contact information:
Jay Armstrong
www.ADaywithJay.com

This book is dedicated to my fabulous family,
without whom literally nothing in my life would be possible.

Special thanks should go to Adam Jones,
who always put up with persistent questions from a first-time author.

The North Texas sun was shining brightly as we rode
along in our Jeep. I was riding in the backseat and having a great
time, but Mom seemed a little nervous.

Today wasn't just any old day—today was my very first day of school! I didn't know why Mom was nervous. I was excited! After all, I was six years old and eager to meet other kids my age.

2

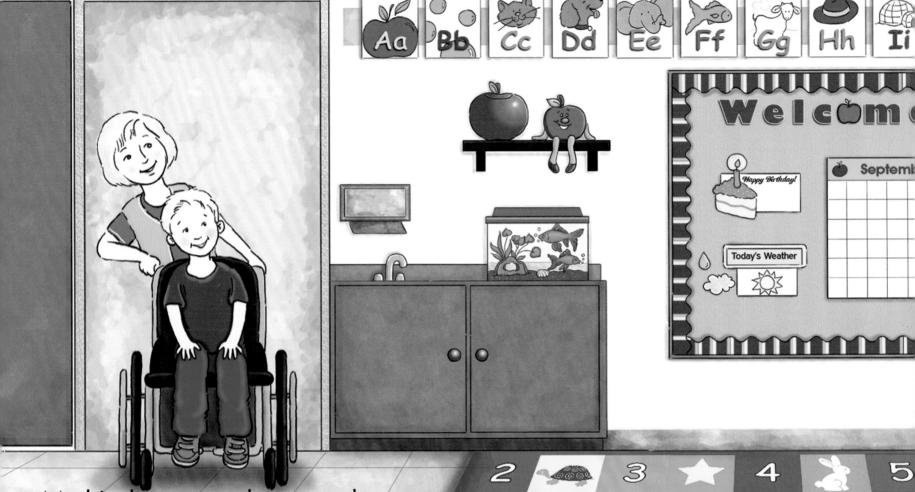

My kindergarten class was the
neatest room I'd ever seen.
It was decorated in warm, bright
colors and had pictures
of letters on the wall.

The floor was covered with a colorful rug that had numbers and letters all over it! I was sitting where Mom had placed me when suddenly, in came a bunch of other children. Most of them looked as excited as I was, but a few of them looked kind of scared.

A loud bell rang. I looked around and saw that my mother was gone. I began to feel a little scared, but then a nice-looking lady appeared at the front of the room.

She said her name was Mrs. May and that she would be our teacher. Her hair was bright red, and she had a very kind smile.

Mrs. May asked all of the students to give their name and say a little something about themselves. Several kids said their names very loudly, while others said them very quietly.

As my turn got closer and closer, I wondered how I would say my name and what I would say about myself. I licked my lips and, trying to sound normal, said, "Hi, I'm Jay. I have a dog named Chance." Phew! Was I glad that was over!

When it was finally time to get up off of the rug, Mrs. May put me back into my wheelchair. I noticed that some of the kids were staring at  me and whispering. I felt as if I wanted to cry. Gosh, what's wrong with me? Then a bell sounded. It was time for lunch.

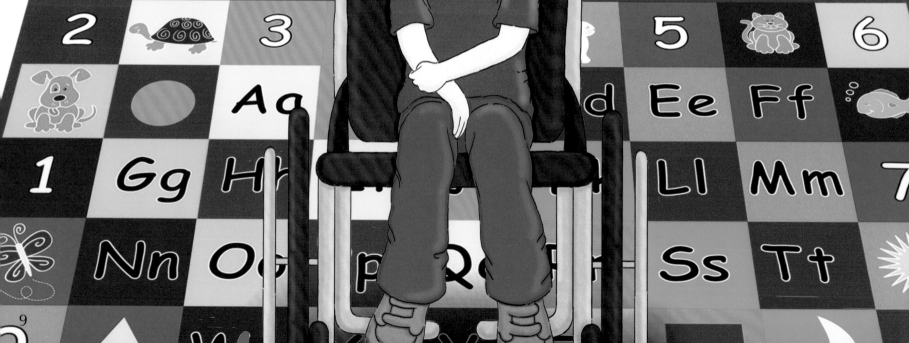

In the hallway after lunch, people were swarming around me and asking me why I was in a wheelchair. I told them I couldn't walk and that the chair helped me to get around.

They all wanted to know why I couldn't walk. "Because I have cerebral palsy," I told them. "What's that?" they asked. I thought and thought and couldn't come up with the right answer. Then, I suddenly remembered my doctor telling me that cerebral palsy made my brain and my legs get their signals mixed up, and that was why I couldn't walk.

I told them how, without even realizing it, the brain sends thousands of signals through the body telling all the different parts what to do. Having cerebral palsy means that your brain isn't sending the right messages to your muscles, which keeps them from working properly.

Just then, Mrs. May called us back to our classroom and said it was time to rest.

Rest time was weird for me. So was sleeping on the floor! But Mom had bought me a brand new green and blue mat just for naps.

As I looked around, I saw my classmates unfolding their mats and placing them on the floor. Someone had even put mine down for me!

"Everyone rest now," said Mrs. May as she flipped
off the lights. The room was dim. The only light shining in was
from behind the curtains and under the door.

My mat smelled like plastic and wasn't nearly as comfortable as my soft bed at home. And Chance wasn't here to sleep with me. This was weird! I felt like talking, but there was no one to talk to—they were all asleep!

Finally, after what seemed like forever, it was
recess time. My classmates stopped asking me
about my wheelchair and started asking me if I played
any sports. "Football!" I told them. "I *love* football!"

How does someone in a wheelchair play football?
Simple! All you need is someone to push you
while the rest of the kids play their positions.

18

The scariest part is trying to not wipe out!
If you do, it's one big CRASH!

After football, it was time to wash up and get ready to go home. My first day of school was over. It was everything I'd hoped it would be! Wow, was I ever happy to see my mom!

If you have classmates who are in a wheelchair or have some other physical challenge, please just be a friend and help them find ways to do the same things that you do. You'll make a great new friend and, who knows, you may even be friends for life!